Copyright

Second published in Great Britain in 2024 by BWF publishing

© Book Writing Founders Publishing Uk, 2024

Text copyright © Sety H., 2024

cover illustration and design, and decorative inside art © Book Writing Founders Uk

Full-page inside illustrations by BWF,

The moral rights of the author has been asserted

All characters and events in this publication other than those in the public domain, are fictitious and any resemblance to real persons, living or dead is purely coincidental.
All rights reserved

No part of this publication may be reproduced, stored in a retrieval system or transmitted in any form or by any means, without the prior permission in writing of the publisher, nor be otherwise circulated in any form of binding or cover other than that in which it is published and without a similar condition including this condition being imposed on the subsequent purchaser.

ISBN: 978-1-962380-935
Book writing founders publishing
86-90 Paul Street, London EC2A 4NE

https://www.bookwritingfounders.co.uk

Our books may be purchased in bulk for promotional, educational, or business use.

Please contact Book writing founders at +44-203-8855296, or by email at mailto: info@bookwritingfounders.co.uk.
Second Edition 2024

Dedication

To all those who need that one
extra cuddle.

Acknowledgement

Has it not been for my two boys, I never would have known what "being needed" really looked like. And how fulfilling and exhausting that could be. Still, I am grateful for experiencing it.

Mommy always
comes back

On a blue planet, in an orange land, on a green street, in a yellow house with a black door lived Bobby and his family.

His mom and dad.
His older brother, Teo.
His slightly older sister, Mimi. And his
funny doggie Lulu.

Bobby loved to jump on the trampoline, play hide-and-seek, and go on walks to explore. But he hated it when his mom had to go away. He was afraid that she wouldn't come back, or even worse that she would forget him.

This, of course, could never be true.
Still, Bobby would get sad when
mom had to leave.

"Mommy always
comes back, Bobby,"
Teo would say and give him a wink.

And sure enough, there she was, coming right back from the grocery store with a smile on her face, just as she always did whenever she saw her kids.

"Mommyyyyyy," Bobby would shout and run toward her as if she had just come back from climbing the highest mountain in the world. (Psst, that's Everest).

"Hi, Bobby! Mommy is here," Mom would always say as she picked him up into a twirl.

And in the morning, when mommy had to go to work, Bobby again would fear she wouldn't come back. "But, buddy, mommy always comes back," Daddy would say and give him a high five and a hug.

And sure enough, just as Bobby was finishing up a high block tower, there she was, coming right back. Ever smiling at Bobby with arms wide, ready to pick him up and give him a kiss.

"Here I am, my darling boy.
**Mommy always
comes back,"**
Mommy never got tired
of saying.

Later that day, as Bobby was running around together with Mimi and Lulu jumping by their side, making a proper mess - Bobby suddenly noticed Mommy was gone.

"Mommy?" He asked with a bit of a sad voice.
"Don't worry, Bobby, mommy always comes back," his sister was quick to reply. "Mommy!" Bobby continued looking around, eyes already filling with tears.

"Mommy is here!" A familiar voice came from behind. Mommy was near, that was clear, and sure enough, there she was, just coming out of the toilet.

Before she could even open the door, Bobby rushed in just to make sure Mommy was actually there. Not a second had passed, and Mimi joined in, drawn by all the ado, just to confirm that all was alright.

This was clearly a job suited for two. Indeed, there was Mommy in the little white room, gleaming with joy. And, wouldn't you know it, here came a THIRD happy guest. Lulu poked her nose, curious to see everyone in that one small, special place.

"Oh, dear, mommy always comes back, didn't you hear?" — Mommy exclaimed with a smile as big as she sun. With one quick move she picked both Mimi and Bobby and carried them playfully onto the couch.

"Never fear, listen, my dear.
Mommy is ALWAYS NEAR." — she
said as she tickled them each.

"And mommy always
COMES BACK!"
Bobby proclaimed, now standing
tall before all, suddenly
GROWN UP so much.

Note to parent

Separation anxiety is a normal part of every child's development, usually occurring three times in the first three years of a child's life.

Please remember, this is related to their underdeveloped nervous system. What they experience is truly quite heavy. Children present clinginess, and sometimes even panic, when you leave the room, but this is not manipulation or play on their part. They are genuinely anxious in these moments.

When the child is treated with patience and kindness during these phases, and when they are consistently reassured, the anxiety also subsides faster. And vice versa, if the child is not met with understanding, the anxiety is fueled and may last longer.

You have done nothing wrong. Your child is not spoiled. You have not 'made them' clingy. It will be okay.

Thank you for your trust. I hope this book has been helpful to you.

I am Sety H, a certified specialist and consultant in positive parenting. If you would like to learn more about its methods, you may download my parenting course for free via the mobile app "Ommm Positive Parenting."

I hope that together we can rediscover the beauty of parenting in our everyday life and add a little bit of magic too.

About the author

Sety H., is a wife, a mother of two boys, a certified positive parenting coach, a linguist, and a quality expert, But most of all is a person with a big compassionate heart that is following her dream of making the world a better place. That dream took roots in her mind during her rough childhood in Bulgaria, Since then she has travelled the world, lived, studied and worked in the US, South Korea, the UK and finally settled down in the Netherlands. In all her travels she kept searching for a way to fulfil that little girl's dream.

Her career progression did not succeed in giving her that answer for a long time. Until the day she became a mother and the Universe opened up a new horizon to her. It was then, in 2015, that she found the power of positive parenting and felt the immediate eliek. It all made sense to her and showed her a clear way of bringing her "happy" in the everyday life, It was also then that she started to write. Her first book was published only a year later, after her son's first birthday. She was on her journey and started to realize the power that parenting brought. The power to make the world a better place. By raising children with love, compassion, kindness and respect she could ensure that flicker of hope. Through her stories and books she started communicating with hundreds of parents, bringing them laughter and comfort in the most challenging times of parenthood. Her first 4 books were written and published only in Bulgaria.

When her second boy was born in the midst of the first lockdown In 2020 everything came into place and Sety finally understood what needed to be done. She signed up for a parenting course, then another and another and got certified as a positive parenting coach, Not long after, in 2021, she published her very own parenting course that was built into a mobile application - Ommm positive parenting. The app is available in three languages (Bulgarian, English and Dutch) and is also the first positive parenting course-app in Bulgarian, With this she could reach thousands of parents worldwide, extending a helping, guiding hand to those who wanted to raise their families with those same values, And this was the only way we could ensure that better world she had always dreamt of.

In 2023, inspired by her two boys, she wrote the children's book series "Bobby's tales of life and wonder", believing her words could bring joy, guidance and magie to both children and parents.

Mommy always comes back

More titles coming to the series:

Bobby and the Circle of Friends
Bobby and the Road of Smiles
Bobby and the Upside-Down World of Dreams
Bobby and the Magic of Animals
Bobby and the Jar of Stars
Bobby and the Soul Firefly
Bobby and the Magical Rainbow

www.ingramcontent.com/pod-product-compliance
Lightning Source LLC
Chambersburg PA
CBHW071444300726

48976CB00004B/1440